Vietnam service medal

A NOTE TO PARENTS

When your children are ready to "step into reading," giving them the right books—and lots of them—is as crucial as giving them the right food to eat. **Step into Reading Books** present exciting stories and information reinforced with lively, colorful illustrations that make learning to read fun, satisfying, and worthwhile. They are priced so that acquiring an entire library of them is affordable. And they are beginning readers with an important difference—they're written on four levels.

Step 1 Books, with their very large type and extremely simple vocabulary, have been created for the very youngest readers. **Step 2 Books** are both longer and slightly more difficult. **Step 3 Books,** written to mid-second-grade reading levels, are for the child who has acquired even greater reading skills. **Step 4 Books** offer exciting nonfiction for the increasingly proficient reader.

Children develop at different ages. **Step into Reading Books,** with their four levels of reading, are designed to help children become good—and interested—readers *faster.* The grade levels assigned to the four steps—preschool through grade 1 for Step 1, grades 1 through 3 for Step 2, grades 2 and 3 for Step 3, and grades 2 through 4 for Step 4—are intended only as guides. Some children move through all four steps very rapidly; others climb the steps over a period of several years. These books will help your child "step into reading" in style!

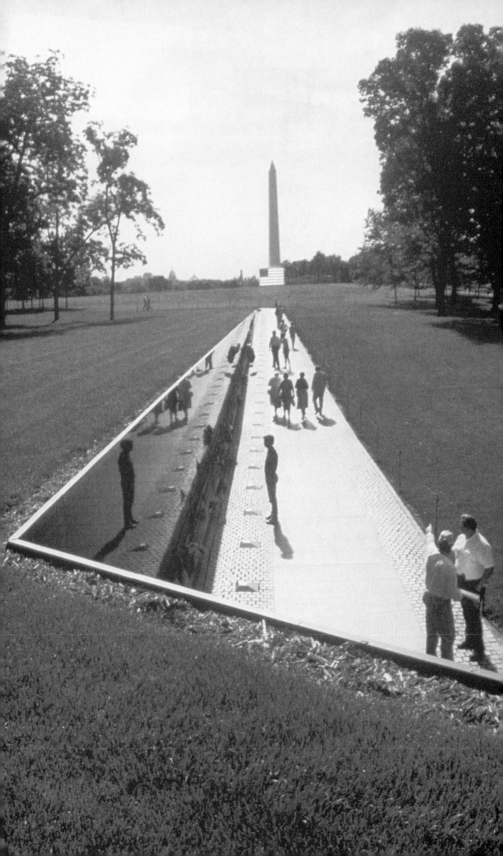

Step into Reading

A WALL OF
◆ NAMES ◆

The Story of the
Vietnam Veterans Memorial

By Judy Donnelly
Illustrated with photographs

A Step 4 Book

Random House 🏠 New York

With thanks to Jan Scruggs for permission to quote from his book *To Heal a Nation,* Harper & Row, Publishers.

Photo credits: pp. 2, 4, 31, 33, 39, William Clark, National Park Service; 6, 15, 24 (bottom), 40, FPG; 7, 48, Friends of the Vietnam Veterans Memorial; 10, 13, 19, 22, 37, AP/Wide World; 20, John Paul Filo; 24 (top), Labbe, 43, Sloan, 45, Bryant, all Gamma Liaison; 28, Globe; 42, UPI/Bettmann.

Cover photo: Seny Norasingh

Photo research by Carousel Research, Inc.

Library of Congress Cataloging-in-Publication Data
Donnelly, Judy. A wall of names: the story of the Vietnam Veterans Memorial/by Judy Donnelly.
p. cm.–(Step into reading. A Step 4 book) Summary: Surveys the history of the Vietnam War, chronicles the construction of the Vietnam Memorial, and discusses what the Memorial means to many Americans. ISBN 0-679-80169-3 (pbk.); ISBN 0-679-90169-8 (lib. bdg.) 1. Vietnam Veterans Memorial (Washington, D.C.)–Juvenile literature. 2. Washington, D.C.–Buildings, structures, etc. –Juvenile literature. [1. Vietnam Veterans Memorial (Washington, D.C.) 2. National monuments. 3. Vietnamese Conflict, 1961–1975.] I. Title. II. Series: Step into reading. Step 4 book.
DS559.83.W18D66 1990
959.704′36–dc20 90-30275

Manufactured in the United States of America 10

STEP INTO READING is a trademark of Random House, Inc.

1

The Wall

It is a sunny afternoon in Washington, D.C. Crowds of people are walking through a park in the center of the city. There are young children holding their parents' hands, teenagers in jeans and sweatshirts, soldiers in uniform, men in business suits.

Some of the people pause by a statue of three young soldiers with sad, tired faces. Then, one at a time, or in small groups, they move down a flagstone path. Now they can see it—the reason they have come

to this place. There, cut into the earth, is a long, shining black wall.

Clouds and sky are reflected in the wall's dark surface. Resting against it are small flags and bunches of flowers, letters and photographs. And names are carved into it—thousands and thousands of names.

As they near the wall, people grow quiet. Some stop and bow their heads. A man reaches out to touch a name. Then he lifts his small son high so he can touch it too. A teenage girl places a red rose near the wall. For a moment she is very still. Then she turns and walks away.

These people are just a few of the visitors who come to the black wall. It is called the Vietnam Veterans Memorial. The names on it belong to all the Americans who died or are still missing in the Vietnam War.

The war was fought in Vietnam, a tiny country in Southeast Asia, thousands of miles away from America. The first

American soldier died there in 1959. By 1975, when the war was finally over, nearly 60,000 Americans had given their lives.

It was the longest war our country ever fought.

It was the only war America ever lost.

It was the most hated war in American history and, to many people, a war America didn't need to fight.

The memorial was built in 1982, nearly ten years after the war was over. It almost didn't get built at all. The Vietnam War had left Americans troubled and angry. Some thought the country was better off without any reminders of this sad and bitter time in our history.

2

The Most Hated War

What was the Vietnam War? Why did Americans disagree about it so bitterly?

It all began after World War Two, in the late 1940s. For many years the small country of Vietnam had been ruled by the French. But the Vietnamese people wanted to rule themselves. They began to fight for their independence. A man named Ho Chi Minh (ho chee MIN) led the fight.

After nine years, Ho Chi Minh won the war for independence. The French

Vietnamese soldiers celebrating their victory over France in 1954.

had to give up their claim on Vietnam. But that did not end the problems for the Vietnamese. Ho Chi Minh and his many followers wanted a Communist government like that of the Soviet Union and China. But some Vietnamese people did not. At a special peace meeting in 1954 an agreement was reached. Vietnam was split into two parts with two separate governments. North Vietnam had a Communist government headed by Ho Chi Minh. South

Vietnam had a government led by a man who was a lifelong foe of communism. His name was Ngo Dinh Diem (NO din yee-EM).

The two parts were supposed to be joined together again. There were supposed to be elections to decide whether the government of the North or the South would rule all Vietnam. But South Vietnam's leaders refused to take part in these elections. Ho Chi Minh was such a popular hero that they were sure he and the Communists would win. Diem and his men did not want to give up power, power that they used to silence anyone who opposed them.

Before long there was trouble. A lot of people in the South did not support their government. They felt it was dishonest and unfair. They believed in Ho Chi Minh and his government. By the late 1950s they had begun to fight against the forces of South Vietnam. These rebels became known as the Viet Cong. North Vietnam sent weapons and soldiers to the Viet Cong. Soon there was all-out war.

The United States decided to help Diem, even though his government was corrupt and unpopular. Fear of communism was the reason the United States took the side it did. At this time American leaders were afraid the Soviet Union might try to take over the whole world. America wanted to stop any country from becoming Communist, even if it was small and faraway, even if its government was bad.

At first the American government just sent war supplies and a few hundred soldiers. These soldiers were called "military advisers." They were not going to fight. They were supposed to help train the South Vietnamese army. There was no fuss about this at home. Most Americans could not even have told you where Vietnam was.

But South Vietnam needed more help. So the United States started sending more money and more men. Years passed and still no victory was in sight for the forces of South Vietnam. So America went a step further–a big step. In 1965 U.S. leaders decided Americans would have to do more

U.S. soldiers landing in Vietnam.

than train South Vietnamese soldiers. Americans would have to fight.

In the beginning only a few thousand soldiers were sent over. But within a few months thousands more were on their way. Did these U.S. forces turn the tide of the war for South Vietnam? No. So America sent more soldiers. By 1966 the number of U.S. troops was up to 200,000. By 1967 over half a million Americans were fighting in Vietnam.

Now every American knew about the Vietnam War. Newspapers were full of stories about it. And television brought the war into millions of American homes. Each night people clicked on their sets and saw nightmarish scenes of battle. There were smoking ruins. American soldiers lay bloody and wounded. Dead bodies were sprawled in the mud. It went on week after week, month after month.

And the war was no closer to ending.

3

The War at Home

As the war in far-off Vietnam dragged on and on, Americans at home began to take sides. Americans who believed in the war were nicknamed "hawks." They agreed with the government. Communism was a threat to the United States. Vietnam must not become a Communist country. No matter what it took, Americans had to keep on fighting.

Americans who wanted the United States to get out of Vietnam were called "doves." Some doves felt that the United

States had no business getting into a war between North and South Vietnam. They wanted the Vietnamese to work out their own problems. Some believed America had nothing to fear from a Communist government in South Vietnam. And they thought it was foolish to support a bad government just because it wasn't Communist. Other doves simply hated the way the war was being fought. Bombs were turning Vietnam into a vast ruin. Chemical weapons were stripping the land of plant life. Worst of all, thousands of innocent people—even children and babies—were being killed when villages were attacked.

The doves wanted to show the American government how they felt about the war. They marched in the streets, chanting and singing and carrying signs that said END THE WAR, STOP THE KILLING, GET OUT OF VIETNAM. Sometimes hawks showed up at these protests with their own signs: USA ALL THE WAY, BOMB NORTH VIETNAM, AMERICA–LOVE IT OR LEAVE IT. Fights often broke out between the two groups.

As the war went on and on, the protests grew bigger and bigger. In 1969 there were meetings and marches against the war in big cities all across America. People stayed home from work to let the government know how much they wanted the war to end. Some protests were held at night. Thousands walked together, each carrying a candle for a soldier who had died in Vietnam. The biggest peace march in history took place in Washington, D.C. As many as 800,000 people came to protest America's part in the Vietnam War.

In 1970 a tragedy occurred during a peace protest. Four college students were shot and killed by special soldiers who were supposed to be keeping order. This

shocked the nation. Over 40,000 American soldiers had died in Vietnam. But now Americans were dying for Vietnam right in their own country.

Every American family with a teenage son was afraid. Would their boy be sent to fight in Vietnam? Would he come back alive? Would this terrible war ever end? America's leaders did not seem to know how to stop it.

America was horrified at the killing of college students during a peace protest.

4

Fighting a No-Win War

What was it like to fight in Vietnam?

For most of the soldiers who fought there, the war was a nightmare.

When a soldier reached Vietnam, he rarely stayed with the buddies he had trained with in America. He was sent to join a group of soldiers who had been fighting together for months. Usually he knew nobody at all.

Many American soldiers were teenagers who had never been away from home before. Now, suddenly, they found themselves in a strange land of rice farms and thatched huts, surrounded by people who spoke a language they could not understand.

South Vietnam was like no place in America. It was covered with swamps and jungles. It was very hot and very wet. It rained a lot of the time. There were biting ants, snakes, and leeches—a kind of worm that attaches itself to people and animals and sucks their blood. It was so different one soldier wrote home, "It's hard to

believe the same stars I see shine down on you."

Still, no matter how hard it was to be there, most American soldiers believed they had come to South Vietnam for a good cause. They were there to help the South Vietnamese people. And they expected the farmers and villagers to be on their side. But that wasn't always true. Some of the farmers wanted the Viet Cong to win. Some were even part of the Viet Cong. To them, the young Americans were the enemy.

Most wars have clearly different sides. The Vietnam War did not. Viet Cong soldiers and ordinary farmers often looked and dressed alike. Sometimes women, old men, and even children helped the Viet Cong. So American soldiers could never be sure whether the Vietnamese people they saw were friends or enemies.

The war was different in other ways too. There were few big battles of one army against another. Instead, small groups of Viet Cong soldiers hid in the jungle or in secret tunnels or in the villages, waiting to attack by surprise. Then they slipped into hiding again.

Most of the time, Americans fought back in small groups. They were sent out on patrols to find enemy soldiers and kill them. Patrols were dangerous. Viet Cong hid in trees or underbrush and shot Americans one at a time. They laid traps and buried bombs. A bomb might be hidden on a footpath or a bridge. One wrong step would set it off.

American soldiers often wondered whether they made any real difference in the war. They might fight for days trying to clear a certain area of enemy soldiers. They would hide in the underbrush dodging bullets and bombs. Their buddies would be wounded or killed. Finally, the gunfire would stop. The enemy had gone. But had the Americans really won? Weeks or even just days later more enemy soldiers would be back.

As time went on, the news from home made it even harder to fight in Vietnam. The soldiers knew that many Americans were against the war. Some even agreed the war was pointless. They heard that U.S. leaders were trying to make peace with North Vietnam. But until they did, the soldiers had to stay and fight and die.

At last, sixteen years after the first American soldier had died in Vietnam, the war finally did come to an end. How did this happen? Most Americans had come to feel the cost of the war was too high—in lives and in money. So, in 1973, the American government signed a peace agreement with North Vietnam and the

Viet Cong. Nearly all the U.S. troops went home that year. The last Americans left in 1975–just as the army of North Vietnam took control of the South.

Sixty thousand Americans had given their lives. More than 300,000 had been wounded. And what the U.S. government had tried to keep from happening had happened anyway. South Vietnam was under Communist rule.

The war was over, but the angry, bitter feelings didn't go away. And it was the returning soldiers who suffered the most from the anger and shame of the American people.

Vietnam veterans did not come back as heroes, like the returning soldiers of other wars. There were no bands to meet them. No parades. Vietnam veterans were ignored. Sometimes soldiers in uniform were even booed or called ugly names.

Many found it impossible to go back

to ordinary life after Vietnam. Vietnam veterans had more problems than soldiers of other wars. Problems with poor health. Problems with drugs. Problems finding jobs. They got less help from the government.

It didn't matter that most Vietnam veterans fought because they had to. It didn't matter how they had suffered. Somehow they were blamed for a war they never made.

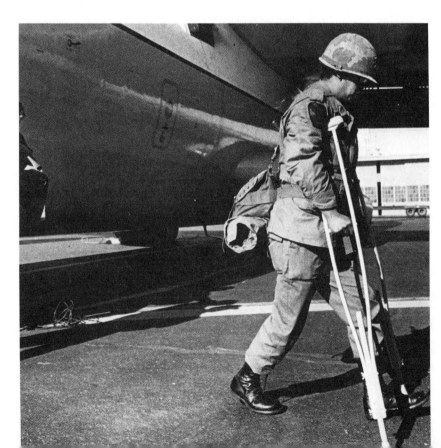

5

All Their Names

It is late one night in 1979. A Vietnam vet named Jan Scruggs sits at his kitchen table.

Jan is one of the lucky ones. He was wounded in Vietnam, but he survived. He came home and made a life for himself. He has a job. He has a wife.

But still, Jan can't forget what it was like to fight in the Vietnam War. Tonight he can't sleep. Over and over again a terrible scene flashes through his mind. A dozen soldiers are unloading a truck.

There is an explosion. Bodies fly through the air. The soldiers are dead and dying. And he stands by, helpless.

It seems like a nightmare, but it is not. It really happened. Those soldiers served with Jan in Vietnam. They were his friends.

Jan keeps thinking of the thousands of others who died in the war. Their country has done nothing to honor them.

He makes up his mind.

He is going to make sure there is a special memorial for the Americans who fought in the Vietnam War. It will list the names of all the men and women who went to Vietnam and never returned—every last one.

Most people think Jan is crazy. What does he know about memorials? It will cost millions of dollars to build one. How will he get the money? Why would Americans want to build a memorial for the Vietnam War anyway? They just want to forget it.

Jan goes right ahead. He holds meetings. He makes speeches. At first no one listens, but then he finds other veterans who like his idea. They agree with Jan that ordinary Americans will want to contribute money to build a memorial. They call themselves the Vietnam Veterans' Memorial Fund.

Newspaper and TV reporters do stories about the fund. Contributions begin to trickle in. A young girl who lost

her father in the war sends ten dollars. A vet with no job sends five. Jan is full of hope, but after two months he has only $144.50. How will he ever be able to raise millions?

There are other problems too. Jan wants the memorial to be for the whole nation. He feels it should stand in the center of Washington, D.C. That means he needs permission from Congress and the president. Why should they listen to him?

Sometimes Jan feels the job is too big. But not for long. A letter always comes along to remind him what a memorial will mean to so many people. Wives and children of vets say how much it helps to know someone cares. Other Vietnam vets tell him they are tired of feeling ashamed about fighting for America. Parents who have lost sons in the war write to thank him for what he is doing. One sends a contribution "in memory of my son, who died after saving the life of his shipmate. He was 18 years old."

After more than a year of trying, something wonderful happens. Jan and the veterans get permission to build a memorial in one of the most important and beautiful places in Washington, D.C. It is in a grassy, tree-lined park between two of America's best-loved places, the Lincoln Memorial and the Washington Monument.

Now the vets are really on their way. People all over America begin to help with the fund-raising. There are tag sales,

concerts, walkathons, parties, and dinners to raise money. Everything from cakes to rifles to prize cows are raffled off.

People want to do something to make up for what had been a terrible time for America. They feel the soldiers who had to fight in Vietnam should be remembered. Maybe in this way something good can come out of the war.

The memorial has become more than the dream of a few veterans. Now it is the goal of thousands of Americans from coast to coast.

6

A Contest

Now that the dream is close to coming true, there is another question.

What will the memorial look like?

The veterans decide to have a nation-wide contest. They choose important artists and builders to judge it. Anyone over 18 years old can submit a design.

Jan's original idea has not been forgotten. So there is one important rule. The memorial must include the name of every American man or woman killed or missing in the war.

The judges receive almost 1,500 designs, many more than they expected. There are so many they can't fit them in an ordinary room. They have to put them in a kind of huge garage for airplanes.

Then they look them over. The judges want to be fair, so no names appear on the designs, only numbers. That way the judges can't tell who the artists are.

They have no problems choosing. Every judge agrees. The best design is the one numbered 1,026.

Who is the winner? Is it a famous artist? A designer of many other memorials?

No! The designer of the winning entry is a college student, a completely unknown 21-year-old woman. Creating a design for the memorial had been a homework assignment. It had gotten a B. She never dreamed that she would win!

The woman's name is Maya Ying Lin. She is Chinese-American. She doesn't

know much about the Vietnam War. She was a baby when America got into it. How did she create the prize-winning design?

Maya says she visited the spot in Washington, D.C., where the memorial was to be built. She stood in the grassy park on a gray November day. She thought about how it must feel to lose someone you love in a war. An idea came to her. She wanted to cut open the earth.

She imagined a black wall standing between the sunny world and the great, dark world beyond that the living can never enter. A great black wall with names on it.

The judges are proud of their choice. So is Jan Scruggs. But some veterans hate the design. Why is it black? Why is it underground? What does it mean? To them it is one more insult for Vietnam veterans. They call it "a black gash of shame." They had expected a statue of brave soldiers in battle, like a famous one that honors the soldiers of World War Two.

These men vow to keep the wall from being built. It seems the veterans will never have a memorial.

Then someone has an idea. Why not have both—Maya Lin's wall and a realistic statue of Vietnam fighting men? This satisfies all the veterans.

Building begins in March 1982. A special stone called black granite is dug out of the mountains of India. It is cut and polished, and then the names are carefully chiseled into the stone, one by one.

Finally, three years after the idea first came to Jan Scruggs, the wall is done.

The Wall was built in less than eight months.

Just as he had dreamed, all the names are there—nearly 60,000 of them. They seem to go on forever.

What had once seemed impossible has really happened. Jan has made it happen. Vietnam veterans will be remembered. They have their memorial.

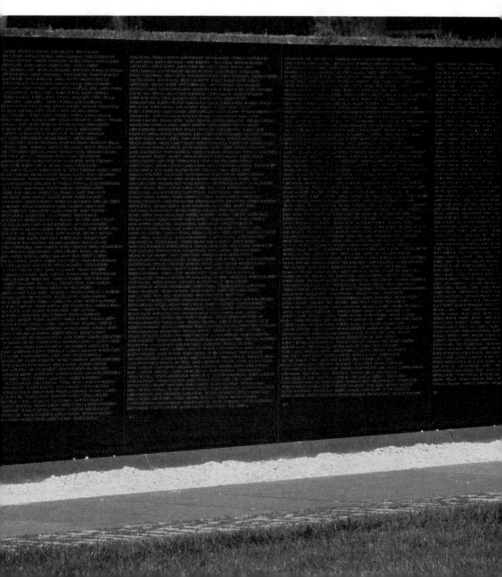

7

Welcome Home

Veteran's Day, November 13, 1982. This is the day that Jan Scruggs and the Vietnam veterans have waited for. Today the memorial will be open to visitors for the first time.

Vietnam vets by the thousands pour into Washington, D.C. Some are in wheelchairs. They wear old army jackets. They pin on their medals. They march in a parade with floats and brass bands in their honor. At last they can feel proud of having fought in Vietnam.

The parade ends near the memorial. Over 150,000 people gather to hear speakers thank the veterans for serving America. Then the fences guarding the wall come down.

The crowd moves toward the wall. Each person searches for a special name that means so much. They reach out. They touch the letters. Some press their lips to the black stone.

Veterans throw their arms around one another. Parents cry over their lost sons. Reporters and newscasters cry just watching them.

The scene is unforgettable. And it appears in newspapers and television broadcasts all over America. This is the homecoming the veterans have wanted for so long.

In the days and weeks that follow, the stream of visitors does not stop. Instead, more and more people come to the wall.

They are there at all hours of the day and night. They come in the chill of winter and in the summer heat.

And something happens that has never happened in the long history of our country or the world.

Visitors to the wall do more than pause and walk away. They leave poems and letters for the dead soldiers. The letters say:

I think of you every day.
It still hurts so much.
I will always love you.

Some of the letters are pages long. They are full of private thoughts, of sad memories and happy ones, of disappointments and dreams. Each one is different and special. "You would have been the most wonderful Daddy in the whole world," a girl writes to her father. "Why

did you die and I live?" one vet asks another.

Sometimes words aren't enough. People leave gifts for the men or women they lost in the war, gifts with special meanings. A mother leaves the teddy bear her son always loved. In a note to him she says, "I thought it should be here with you." A photograph of a smiling child is scribbled with a message: "I wanted you to see how beautiful your little boy is."

Every day park rangers seem to find something new. An army medal. A harmonica. A can of maple syrup.

What makes people leave gifts and letters at the wall? There is no single answer. Many of the people who do it find it hard to explain themselves. But they all say that here at the wall they feel close to their loved ones. "I think my son hears and understands," one mother says.

Jan Scruggs has thought a lot about the wall. He believes that for years people kept their sad feelings about the war inside. The wall helps them to say good-bye.

Maya Lin puts it another way. She believes that a visit to the wall is like a journey back in time. That is why she wanted the names arranged by date of death—day by day, month by month, year by year. Finding the name of a special woman or a man who died means going back to that terrible moment. It means facing the loss. That is the beginning of healing.

Many people say the wall is helping to heal the entire nation.

The Vietnam War divided Americans. But the memorial brings everyone together again. It is for the living and for the dead.

It honors all the men and women who never came back from Vietnam. It helps everyone who loved them.

It makes the veterans who survived the war feel like part of the country again.

It even helps the millions who had been against the war. As one woman says, "It is so sad to see all those names and think of the lives cut short, the families left broken-hearted. I just hope the wall will make us stop and think before we send our boys off to die again."

Does the wall have meaning for the rest of the world? Yes. Anyone who loves a parent, a child, a husband, a brother, a sister, or a friend can understand it. It says pain, sorrow, loss—that is the price of war.

The wall is not just about war. It's about the love that goes on after death. The love that is our best hope for peace.